Billy Angel

Sam Hay

Illustrated by Emma Dodson

A & C Black • London

First published 2008 by
A & C Black Publishers Ltd
38 Soho Square, London, W1D 3HB

www.acblack.com

Text copyright © 2008 Sam Hay
Illustrations copyright © 2008 Emma Dodson

The rights of Sam Hay and Emma Dodson to be
identified as the author and illustrator of this work respectively
have been asserted by them in accordance with the
Copyrights, Designs and Patents Act 1988.

ISBN: 978-0-7136-8881-8

A CIP catalogue for this book is available from the British Library.

This book is produced using paper that is made from wood grown in
managed, sustainable forests. It is natural, renewable and recyclable.
The logging and manufacturing processes conform to the
environmental regulations of the country of origin.

Printed and bound in Great Britain by Cox and Wyman Ltd.

chapter 1

Plumbing. That's what the future had in store for me. From as early as I can remember, and even before that, I knew I was destined to spend my life with my arm stuck down someone else's toilet. And to be totally honest, I wasn't very happy about it.

'Happy Birthday, Billy.'

That's me, age three, with a plunger on my head and a set of plastic plumbing tools on my lap. See how cheesed-off I look. That's because what I really wanted was a bright-yellow, shiny digger, like my best friend Barry's.

'Happy Birthday, Billy.'

There I am again. I'm the small boy standing in front of 2,000 new toilets. Yes, *2,000 toilets*. I'm six and it's my birthday treat – a visit to the toilet factory. I look ecstatic, don't I?

Oh, and that's me again. It's Christmas and I'm the one holding the giant book that doesn't quite fit on my lap. I'm eight and the book is *The A to Z of Practical Plumbing Problems*. Don't laugh. That's really what I got for Christmas that year. It may look like I'm smiling, but inside I'm seething.

You see my dad, William Box, is a plumber, just like his father before him and his father before him and his father before him. In fact, if you could be bothered going right back to the beginning of time, you'd probably find a William Box in a loin cloth up to his arm in dinosaur doo-doo sorting out someone's cesspit problems.

I'm called William Box, too. But despite the name and millions of years of tradition, I've always known plumbing wasn't for me. I have absolutely no interest in pipes. Or poo. Or blocked sinks. Or smelly drains. Or leaky radiators. Or bothersome ball cocks. The only

6

trouble is, I haven't quite worked out how to tell my dad. Or my mum, for that matter.

You see, Mum's almost as potty about plumbing as Dad. She says she's a social historian, but all she's really interested in is how Joe Bloggs back in eighteen-something or other washed his shorts or took a whiz.

She's currently building a matchstick-model replica of the original London sewer system. It's got flushing lavs and everything. It's enough to make you weep.

My parents talk endlessly about plumbing. They dream about plumbing. They watch plumbing programmes on TV. They read plumbing magazines. They go on holiday with other plumbers. They even crack plumbing jokes, which are not funny.

'What do you call a highly skilled plumber?'

'A drain surgeon.'

No, I didn't laugh, either.

And that's what I thought my destiny was. A lifetime of dreadful jokes and endless blocked loos. But I was wrong. Fate had something *far* stranger in store for me.

chapter 2

It was the eve of my eleventh birthday and life was about to go down the pan. Completely!

As usual, I was looking forward to a pile of pointless plumbing presents (PPPs), which I'd stuff under the bed along with all the others.

If you ever find yourself desperately searching for a pair of polyester pyjamas with purple pliers on them, I can help you out.

Maybe you're itching to read about the history of the automatic washing machine, with extra diagrams and full-colour photos. If so, give me a call.

But crap presents were the least of my worries this year. Because I was about to turn eleven. That might not sound like a big deal to you. But to a Box it's a big occasion. You see, destiny calls us Boxes on the eve of our eleventh birthdays. And that destiny is always plumbing.

It happened to my dad, his brothers, and Grandad, too.

They'll all tell you the same story: the night before they turned eleven, just as they were drifting off to the land of nod, they had the weirdest dream. A shaft of golden light appeared from the ceiling, there was a faint pong of plumber putty, and suddenly a life of smelly sinks and dirty drains beckoned to them.

That was all it took. They got up the next day as though a whopping great water tank had burst in their brains, flooding out any other thoughts apart from plumbing.

Yeah, that's what I thought, too. A load of codswallop, with the distinct smell of last month's Camembert. But it's true. That's how it happens in my family. Wham! Bham! Your life's down the pan. Happy eleventh birthday.

So you'll understand how excited I was to go to bed the night before I turned eleven.

Yeah, not very.

'Goodnight, son, and the best of British,' said Dad, clenching his fist in a manly gesture of encouragement, as I slunk up to bed wearing my spanner-shaped slippers. (Another PPP.)

'Sleep well, sweet dreams,' giggled Mum, as she switched off my light.

9

But actually I wasn't too worried because, unknown to them, I had a plan. There was no way I was going to Dream the Dream.

As soon as Mum had gone, I snuck out of bed and put on my football kit. The whole shebang: boots, shin pads, socks and all. Then I climbed back into bed clutching my football in one hand and my box of *Goal!* back issues in the other.

You see, I'm planning to be an international footballer. Not a plumber – international or otherwise. And I reckoned that if I dressed the part, it might make me dream of football. *Not plumbing.*

For a long time I couldn't sleep. I was trying so hard *not* to think about plumbing that all I could think about *was* plumbing. But eventually I must have dropped off because the next thing I remember was the football rolling off my bed and waking up with a start.

I blinked at the clock.

3:03 am.

Had I escaped my destiny? I couldn't remember Dreaming the Dream. And I certainly wasn't swinging from the light at the thought of bleeding a radiator.

I sighed deeply, lay back on my pillows and closed my eyes with a smug smile of satisfaction.

And that's when I heard it…

'William Box? Are you William Box?'

I sat bolt upright.

'Only the address isn't very clear. And I haven't got much time.'

I gasped.

Standing at the bottom of my bed was a thuggish-looking bloke. If I'd seen him on the street, I'd have crossed the road. He was tall and mean-looking, in a hooded top and jeans. His nose was squashed, and his hair looked like a loo brush. But the weirdest thing was the light. All around him was a white light, sunglasses bright. It hurt to look.

A rush went through my brain: was it a burglar? Or a mad axeman?

'What do you want?' I squeaked, shading my eyes and clutching my football mags, in case he made a grab for them.

But he wasn't listening. He was peering at a scrap of paper.

'William Box, 15 Lavender Rise?' he muttered to himself. 'Lavender Rise? What sort of stupid, girly sounding address is that anyway?'

Suddenly I felt cross, despite myself. The fact that some spiky weirdo in a translucent, hooded top was standing at the bottom of my bed somehow seemed less important than my street name being ridiculed.

'What's wrong with Lavender Rise?' I said.

'What's *right* with it?' he snapped. 'But who cares what sort of frilly street you live in. Are you William Box or not?'

I was still cross, but I nodded.

That seemed to please him, because he dropped the paper and stepped forward with a sort of twisted smile on his face.

And that's when an awful thought smacked me on the chops. Maybe I was actually asleep. Could this be something to do with Dreaming the Dream? Was this bloke about to tell me my future was toilet-shaped?

'Look,' I said desperately. 'If this is anything to do with plumbing, I don't want to know…'

He frowned.

'…Because, I am *not* going to be a plumber – not ever! So if you're anything to do with Dreaming the Dream, or toilets, or central-heating systems, I'm not interested. Not in the slightest. Now, please go away.'

I dived under the duvet and held my breath.

But he didn't go away.

Suddenly, I felt a pointy finger poking my head through the covers.

'Look, squirt,' he growled. 'I haven't got all night. I've no idea what you're wittering on about, but I'm here with a message, so stop messing around and listen.'

Reluctantly, I peeped out. He was standing right next to my bed. 'You're too bright,' I said, squinting in the light, 'and you smell funny.'

But he didn't smell of plumbing putty. It was something much fouler, like burnt anchovies or grilled-sardine sandwiches.

He frowned. Then suddenly he dulled down a little, like a TV that had just had its brightness adjusted. He cleared his throat and shuffled his feet, looking slightly embarrassed. 'The thing is, you've been chosen. Your destiny is mapped out. You are to become…'

I clasped my hands over my ears. 'I DON'T WANT TO BE A PLUMBER!' I yelled.

'…an angel,' he said firmly.

'A *what*?' I hadn't heard him. But somehow I knew he hadn't said plumber.

'An angel!' he growled impatiently.

The first thing I thought was: YES! No blocked bogs for me. But then I realised what he'd actually said.

An *angel*?

'Don't worry; you're not dead or nothing. Not yet, anyway…' he chortled to himself.

I noticed he was missing a few teeth.

'I can't be an angel,' I squeaked. I thought of all the angels I knew. There was the plastic one we stuck on our Christmas tree each year. She wore a pink, frilly dress and had golden,

14

curly hair. I looked nothing like her. Thank God. And then there were the ones in the school nativity play. Always girls. Always *sappy* girls, with sappy wings. Lads were *never* angels.

'Angels are just for girls,' I said.

He glared at me. 'No, they aren't.'

I suddenly noticed he had two rather large, white, feathery things stuck to his shoulders.

Wings?

Angel wings?

I'd clearly put my foot in it, which probably meant I was about to get a bashing from an oversized budgie.

But he didn't bash me. He just scowled, and then I realised he was counting to ten.

I held my breath in case he was still cross when he got to the end.

But he wasn't.

When he stopped counting, he took a deep breath. 'You are to be a guardian angel on Earth and your job is to protect people.'

'Protect them from what?' I had a vision of pushing people out of the way of fast moving cars or falling pianos...

'Themselves, usually,' said the heavenly hoodie, glumly.

'But aren't guardian angels supposed to appear from heaven?' I spluttered. 'I mean, in all the movies, they aren't real people, they're, well, sort of dead ones with wings. A bit like you, I suppose.'

'There's a shortage in heaven,' said the bloke. 'They've already scraped the bottom of the barrel up there.'

Charming.

'Now listen. Your first mission is to protect a girl called Thelma Potts.'

Thelma Potts... The name hung in the air like the pong from a particularly whiffy loo. I knew her from school. Her family owned Potts Pies – a shop selling 300 different varieties of pie. She looked like an upside-down triangle, with a spew of brown, frizzy hair that stuck out everywhere. She was five years older than me, and 500 times bigger. She was the town Judo champ. *And* she had four big brothers who all resembled Great Apes. Thelma Potts was the *last* person who needed protecting.

I gulped. And I tried to protest, but the big bloke wasn't listening.

'You are to protect Thelma from her dark side.'

'*What*?' I squeaked. 'What are you *talking* about?'

'Thelma Potts is in danger. Your mission is to stay close to her, and protect her from harm. That's it!' he said. 'Message delivered. Sign here, please.' He produced a sheet of paper and a white pencil.

I folded my arms. 'No,' I said firmly. 'I will not. I don't want to be an angel. And I certainly don't want to be Thelma Potts' angel.'

Suddenly, I was blinded by the white light again. He'd slapped it back up to full beam.

'You have no choice,' he thundered. 'SIGN!'

And so I did.

The hoodie-angel didn't speak again; he simply vanished into my wardrobe.

For five minutes I didn't do anything. I just sat there blinking, as my eyes readjusted to the darkness. Then, gingerly, I crept over to the wardrobe and peaked inside…

He had gone!

Completely.

Well, not quite. I picked up a single, white feather that was lying on the floor. I wondered whether it was from the spare pillow in the top of my wardrobe or from the scary, hoodie-angel that had spent the last ten minutes terrorising me. Then I crept back into bed, and tried desperately to Dream the Dream. I decided that being a plumber was far more appealing than being an angel. But no matter how hard I tried, it didn't happen.

And as the sun rose on my eleventh birthday, I realised just how far down the pan my life had actually gone.

chapter 3

This is probably the point where I should tell you a bit about myself.

Well, I'm small and skinny. I've got black hair that sticks out at the back. I like football, and maps. I don't like quiche. Or rice pudding, or singing. My best friend is called Barry.

And I'm not an angel.

It's impossible. I'm not even that good at helping people. I hate the sight of blood. I can't bear it when anyone blubs. And I'm not brave. Not in the slightest. So all this angel stuff was bonkers. Someone, somewhere had obviously made a big mistake. A big, fat, super-sized mess-up.

Anyway, I tried not to think about it as I padded downstairs that morning.

I knew they'd be waiting for me. I put it off for as long as I could, but eventually I knew I had to face them.

'He's coming!' I heard Mum shriek. 'Now,

remember, Willie – no pressure, let him tell you in his own time.'

And there they were, trying to look casual at the kitchen table. They'd obviously been up for hours, biting their nails to find out whether I'd Dreamed the Dream. There were piles of newspapers and empty plates on the table. And the stress was showing.

Dad was pretending to read his favourite plumbing mag: *Bleeding Radiators*. (I promise you, that's what it's called.) Except it was upside down and I could see his hands were shaking.

Mum was buttering both sides of a bit of toast. 'Happy Birthday, son,' she dropped the toast and hugged me tight.

'This is for you, lad,' said Dad, pointing to an oddly shaped parcel wrapped in purple paper with pictures of taps all over it. (You're probably wondering where my parents get all their weird plumbing stuff – the cards... the wrapping paper... Yeah, I know it's not in the shops you go to, but trust me, plumbers live in a world of their own. They shop in different shops to the rest of us. And believe me; you do *not* want to go there.)

I sat down and tried to summon up the

enthusiasm to open the parcel. I sighed and half-heartedly pawed at the paper.

'You look tired, love,' smiled Mum.

'Too many dreams, eh, son?' chirped Dad.

I grimaced, and Dad's eyes lit up. He obviously assumed it had happened. That I'd spent the night dreaming of leaky pipes and blocked bogs. I wanted to scream, 'I didn't Dream the blinkin' Dream, all right! I'm not going to be a plumber (though I may be an angel).'

But I didn't. Largely because by now I'd managed to convince myself that last night's nightmare was just that – a nightmare. Not real. Of *course* it couldn't be real. So, instead, I concentrated on unwrapping my gift.

'It's, er… brilliant, Dad!' I said trying to sound sincere.

It was a leather tool bag. A big blighter. The type of bag you'd expect a superhero plumber to have if your boiler had exploded and was spewing boiling-hot water over your entire family, and he'd just flown in to sort it out. This bag could definitely save the day, probably all by itself. It *was* brilliant, if you're as potty about plumbing as my dad is.

21

'Look inside, son,' said Dad excitedly. 'They're all engraved with your initials.'

It was like a Tardis in there. Tools. Tools. And, er, more tools. There were big ones. Bigger ones. And truly mammoth-sized ones. There were at least six different spanners. Piles and piles of pliers. Three hacksaws and a plunger. Plus hundreds of dangerous-looking implements I didn't recognise at all.

'I don't know what to say, Dad.'

I genuinely didn't.

But it didn't seem to matter, because the next thing I knew I was sandwiched between Mum and Dad in an emotional embrace.

'Welcome to the business, son.'

'We're so proud of you.'

And that was that. Angel or not. I was now William Box Esquire: trainee plumber.

Of course I wasn't *really* a trainee plumber. Not yet. This isn't *Oliver Twist*. Children don't go up chimneys any more. Nor do they begin their plumbing apprenticeships aged eleven. I was still allowed to go to school and have a life of sorts. But there was no doubt about it – my course was set.

For the time being, I decided to lump it. After all, there wasn't much else I could do. It was the start of the holidays. And Mum and Dad were strict stickers to the 'no graft, no pocket money' rule. So, as usual, I was set to spend my summer helping Dad, when I'd much rather have been out playing footie with my mates.

It's not that bad, I suppose. I just carry the tools and shake my head and sigh along with Dad when he arrives at a job. And he does pay me. (The fact that I'm secretly saving for soccer school is strictly between you and me.)

Anyway – after what felt like three days listening to Dad droning on about each tool in turn: explaining its merits, uses and complete unabridged history, the phone rang... And rang... And rang. Until Dad finally stopped talking long enough to answer it.

I helped myself to a bowl of cornflakes.

Dad was on the phone for ages. I noticed he was sighing and nodding, and tutting and puffing, which no doubt meant it was an emergency plumbing problem. Dad's favourite. They're usually the most complicated, and they make the most money.

I stopped listening and instead concentrated on my cornflakes. I was just about to stuff a huge spoonful into my mouth when...

'No problem, Mr Potts, the lad and I will be round within the hour.'

Potts! Dad said *Mr Potts*! Surely it could not be Thelma Potts' *dad*? I froze. Then I cursed myself. Potts was a common enough name. I chuckled softly, then stuffed the cornflakes in.

I shouldn't have.

'Yes, I know exactly where your shop is,' Dad was chortling: 'You can't exactly miss it. Not with that three-foot pie outside.'

Three-foot pie?
POTTS' PIES!

I gasped. A tunnel of air sucked the cornflakes down my windpipe. And for a second or two I couldn't breathe. I think I may have turned blue, because Dad suddenly dropped the phone and dived across the kitchen to give me a hearty clatter on the back, which ejected the cornflakes from my mouth like a cork out of a bottle.

'Don't eat so fast,' he scolded, as I collapsed coughing on the floor. 'Sorry, Mr Potts, my apprentice was acting up. We'll be there soon. And yes, I'll ask for your daughter, Thelma.'

I was still collapsed in a coughing fit, with my head spinning.

Thelma Potts?

Thelma Potts!

The face of the hoodie-angel burst into my brain, and I suddenly felt rather peculiar, like someone had just stuck ice cubes under my armpits. Stay calm, I told myself. This is not a sign. It's a coincidence. *I am not an angel!*

Dad didn't seem to notice my inner turmoil. He was grinning his excited plumber grin. The one he wears when a particularly nasty plumbing problem appears...

25

'Come on, Billy, grab your bag. You're going to love this one.'

I was not. If only Dad knew how little I would love this one, perhaps he wouldn't have been grinning quite so much.

chapter 4

We left straight away. Both of us armed. One of us dangerous! Watch out, sewage systems, William Box Jr has been unleashed. And he now comes fully equipped with his own set of scary tools.

Dad didn't seem worried.

'I love Potts' pies,' he was saying. 'I wonder if they'll pay us in pies?'

I tried to laugh. But it got stuck in my throat, which was still sore from the cornflakes incident.

Dad prattled on about pies and pipes and double-trap siphonic pans. (That's a type of toilet, in case you're interested.)

As usual I switched off at the slightest mention of anything to do with plumbing. Instead, I was mentally preparing for meeting Thelma Potts. You see, I probably should have told you earlier. Thelma Potts and I have a bit of a history… There'd been a rather nasty incident a few months ago at the school play.

It was a production of *Peter Pan*. And everyone was involved. For some bizarre reason, Thelma had decided she wanted to play Tinkerbell. And as no one ever argues with Thelma Potts, Tinkerbell she became. Anyway, it was opening night and, amazingly, everything was going swimmingly. The actors were on stage doing their opening number, Thelma was charming the pants off the audience as Tinkerbell (the biggest fairy in fairyland), and me and Barry were sitting behind the stage ready for the set change (we'd been roped in as scenery hands). Then all of a sudden, Mr Fothergill the music teacher appeared, all sweating and worried-looking.

'Quick, laddie,' he whispered. 'Captain Hook's got stage fright and is refusing to go on.'

For one extremely scary moment I thought he wanted me to go on in his place. I found myself edging behind Barry in a 'No! Please! Take him' sort of a manoeuvre.

But as usual I'd got the wrong end of the stick.

Mr Fothergill was taking off his glasses and inserting a hook up his sleeve. 'I've got to take his place,' he gasped, tying a cape around his shoulders. 'So one of you will have to work the pulley for Tinkerbell.'

We gulped. Being in charge of hoisting Thelma Potts up to the ceiling for her flying fairy scene was a major responsibility. Thelma was the scariest girl in the school. She was widely suspected of having eaten the school gerbil when she was six. But we didn't have a choice. Mr Fothergill was now a fully fledged pirate. And you don't argue with a man with a hook for a hand.

He ushered us over to the pulley. 'You've seen it done loads of times, boys,' he whispered.

I bit my lip. Barry and I never paid attention in rehearsals. They had always just been a good excuse to get out of doing something else.

'Remember,' he said. 'Pull it up for down, and down for up. And be gentle,' he added, before sweeping on to the stage to a chorus of *boos!* from the audience.

Barry and I looked at each other. What on earth was he talking about? Up was down, and down was up? It sounded like a dance. And then suddenly we heard Tinkerbell's music begin. This was it. This was when she was supposed to fly above Captain Hook's head...

Barry and I froze, then someone stuck their head around the curtain and pointed upwards. And we went for it. Both of us. We lunged at the lever and moved it the only way it would go – downwards. But with two of us doing it, and all our nervousness, we were a bit too enthusiastic.

We heard a shriek and a scream from the stage area. And then Thelma appeared above the top of the stage curtain. Way, way too high. She was looming over the hall like a hairy pterodactyl. There was a clunk as she bumped her head on the ceiling lights.

'My hair's on fire!' she screamed. (A total exaggeration, as it was only slightly singed at the ends.)

'Down!' someone yelled. 'Get her down.'

We were so shocked at what we'd done, that we both let go of the lever and… *Crash*! Thelma dropped like a stone and landed, with a thud, right on top of Captain Hook. It was lucky she did, seeing as she'd fallen from quite a height. It might have been much worse otherwise. Yours truly may well have been writing this from the clink for first-degree murder. But Mr Fothergill didn't see it as lucky. He was lying in a crumpled heap, groaning softly.

There was pandemonium. Ambulances were called. The fire brigade arrived. And Thelma had to be restrained from braining Barry and me. We were given a police escort home. For our own protection.

So a hoodie-angel appearing in my room saying that I was supposed to protect Thelma Potts was just ridiculous. Heck! – It was *me* that needed a guardian angel – for protection from *her*.

chapter 5

We'd hardly stepped inside Potts' Pie Emporium when Thelma clocked me. Eyes blazing, she'd sprung over the counter and come at me, pie slice in hand.

'You!' she spat the word like a snake spitting venom at its prey. 'You're the one who tried to kill me.'

Even Dad momentarily lost his smug-plumber smile.

Thelma towered over both of us, and I felt myself shrinking beneath her murderous glare.

'Give me one good reason why I shouldn't slice and dice you,' she bellowed.

'Because if you do, you'll never get your sinks unblocked,' laughed Dad, who'd obviously decided this was all harmless horseplay from joshing school chums...

With her pie slice still pointing in my direction, Thelma turned on him. 'Are you the plumber?'

Dad put out his hand. 'William Box, at your service.'

Slowly, she lowered the pie slice and nodded to a swing door at the back of the shop. 'Through there! Grant the pie chef is waiting for you.'

Dad nodded cheerfully, swung his bag over his shoulder and followed his nose. Literally. Because coming from that direction was a stink that could have floored a skunk. Even a brainless bloke like me with a totally untrained nose could tell that Potts' Pie Emporium had a major plumbing problem on its hands. And for once I was extremely glad I was part of the solution. It meant I had a good excuse to put some distance between the scary pie slice and myself.

Dad sniffed manfully, his nose analysing the pong, rolled up his sleeves and headed for the three stainless-steel sinks to the rear of the kitchen.

A small, spotty youth was already there, pouring green gunge down the plugholes. 'It's just making it worse,' he said. 'I've no idea what's causing it.'

This was obviously Grant the pie chef. 'I've never smelled anything like it,' he said with a worried expression.

Dad shook his head. 'Stop the caustic soda, son, and let me take a look.'

There are moments when I am extremely proud of my dad. When everyone is at the end of their tether and he shows up at a job with his big bag of tools and his head full of answers, I feel my chest swell and my chin jut out. Suddenly, you can keep your brain surgeons and astronauts. My dad's the *real* hero. But unfortunately these moments never last.

'Billy! Stop gawping and get me an eight-foot auger and a force cup.'

What? What's he on about? As usual, I'm clueless, and Dad has to speak in pidgin plumber. 'You know; the long, metal rope and the black, rubbery plunger thing.'

And then I know, beyond doubt, that I will never, no matter how hard I try, never ever become a plumber.

After five minutes, I stopped noticing the smell. It hadn't gone anywhere. But I'd sort of acclimatised. Though not everyone had...

'How long is this going to take?' Thelma burst through the shop door and stood scowling in the doorway, pie slice in hand. 'I'm losing customers in droves.'

Dad shook his head. 'There's a major blockage in your pipe work. I've unscrewed the trap and it's not local…'

Thelma frowned. She was obviously as rubbish with the technical jargon as I was.

'I'll have to clear the main drain,' said Dad. 'Which is a big job.'

Thelma rolled her eyes. 'Then I'm shutting up shop. I can't sell pies in a place that smells like someone's died in it.' (I noticed she glared at me as she said the bit about 'died'.) She folded her arms. 'So, how long will it take to sort out?'

'Depends on where the blockage is,' said Dad, who was refusing to be intimidated by a 16-year-old schoolgirl.

'Well, it needs to be fixed by tomorrow,' snapped Thelma. 'Or we're really in the smelly brown stuff.'

Grant smiled sheepishly. 'It's the bi-annual Potts' pie-eating competition tomorrow,' he explained.

'The what?' I asked stupidly.

'What cave do you live in!' barked Thelma. 'We're famous for our pie-eating contest.

We've got competitive eaters coming from all over the world, and if this kitchen isn't back to full working order by then, we're all going to be in big trouble.'

By the way she was boggling me, I sensed I might be in the biggest trouble of all.

'We'll do our best,' said Dad sternly. 'But in the world of blocked drains, there are no guarantees.'

With a giant sigh and a toss of her hair, Thelma turned tail and stalked back to the shop.

I looked up to see Grant staring after her with a goofy look on his face.

'Is she always that unfriendly,' said Dad as he put away his plunger.

'Not when you get to know her,' said Grant softly.

I suddenly realised what was going on.

Grant the pie chef had the hots for Thelma!

It was impossible! How could he? How could *anyone*? I felt quite queasy at the thought.

'Thelma's going through a tough time at the moment,' said Grant, almost to himself.

I found myself asking, 'Why?'

'Because she's just had her heart broken by a no-good low-life, who deserves a good thumping, if you ask me.' Grant's face looked mean.

'Who broke her heart?' (What was I doing? Why did I care?)

'The Pitt!' growled Grant. 'You know – Charlie 'the Pitt' Pittam – the champion sausage swallower.'

'The *what*?' I was becoming genuinely interested now.

'He's one of the competitors in the pie-eating competition. He already holds the world record for swallowing 17 sausages in six minutes, and now he plans on smashing the pie-eating record tomorrow night. Or was, before we had this trouble…'

'But why did he break Thelma's heart?'

'Because he played her along for free pies,' explained Grant. 'He's been in training for this contest for six months. And all that time he's been dating Thelma and benefiting from free pies to practise with. But a week before the contest, when he's all ready to win it, he drops her like a stone and takes up with one of the Skinner sisters.'

I didn't need to ask who, because Grant was obviously on a roll.

'…you know, Selina Skinner, heir to the Skinner Sausage Empire, and host of the next competitive eating contest after ours.'

I'd heard enough. It was all too silly for words.

'This Charlie bloke sounds like a bit of a rotter,' said Dad, taking out an enormous pair of pliers.

'He is. But don't worry, Mr Box. He'll get what he deserves.' Grant was visibly squaring up, and the whites of his knuckles were showing through clenched fists.

'Calm down,' I said. 'Thelma doesn't need anyone to fight her battles for her.' (Certainly not a skinny pie chef and an eleven-year-old trainee plumber!) 'It's that Charlie bloke I feel sorry for,' I added. 'Because when Thelma gets her hands on him, I don't rate his chances.'

And then suddenly the hoodie-angel's face burst into my brain: *Your job is to protect Thelma Potts from her dark side: protect her from herself.*

I felt a strange nipping sensation around my ears, as though I was being attacked with a clothes peg, and I shuddered. Surely Thelma wasn't really planning on doing this bloke in?

chapter 6

There was plenty of stuff Thelma could use. The kitchen was fitted out like a torture chamber with mincers, pincers, pie slices, and a whole wall of sharp knives and choppers. Plus there was the giant, walk-in baking oven at the back. Ten minutes in that thing would sort Charlie Pittam out. For ever!

'Come on, Billy.' Dad was packing up. 'Grant's going to show us the main drain outside.'

I carried the tool bags, but my brain wasn't really on the job any more. Instead, I kept picturing poor Charlie Pittam being sliced and diced and baked in a pie by Thelma Potts.

The drain was in the alleyway outside the shop. It was covered in muck and dirt, but no match for my dad. In minutes, he'd heaved it open and was shining his torch down below. The stench was unbelievable.

Dad put on some serious-looking gloves, then reached down into the hole. After wrestling

39

with the big chunk of pipe for a few minutes, he managed to crack it open. Then…

'Blimey!' he gasped.

I'd never seen my dad shocked by anything before. When it comes to plumbing, he's seen it all, done it all and even appeared in several extremely dull information films on the subject. (Seriously: there's a video available at B&Q entitled 'Learning to Love Your Gas-fired Central Heating System', starring my dad.)

Grant and I leant forward.

'Get me a bucket,' gasped Dad. 'And make it a big one.'

As Grant scuttled off, I wondered whether Dad wanted to throw up, as the stench was now unbearable.

'Fish eyes!' gasped Dad. 'There's a ton of 'em down here.'

Fish eyes?

'There can't be,' said Grant, who'd returned carrying a huge metal bin. 'We don't use much fish, and what we do comes pre-prepared – gutted and headless.'

'See for yourself.'

I shivered as Dad slopped a handful of bloody gunge into the pail. I didn't really want to look. But somehow I couldn't help myself. And sure enough, there, staring up at me, were hundreds of tiny eyes. Small, startled and blood-covered. They were totally gross. I felt a barf coming and sensibly stepped back.

Chefs are obviously made of stronger stuff, because Grant was peering into the slop as though it was something extremely interesting.

'This is weird stuff,' he said shaking his head. 'I must talk to Thelma…'

'Thelma?' I gasped. What had Thelma got to do with fish eyes?

'Thelma's been borrowing the kitchen a lot recently to work out new recipes for the shop. But fish-eye pie… mmm, I'm not sure that would be a winner with the customers.'

I grimaced, imagining biting into a pie and finding myself chewing on a mouthful of chunky fish eyes. What on earth was Thelma thinking of?

'There's loads of hair, too,' said Grant. 'And aren't those feet?'

'Feet?' Dad peered in.

'Yeah – they look like frogs' feet, or something…'

It was all too much for me. Eyes! Hair! Feet!

'I'll just go and get us some drinks from the café…'

And before Dad could argue, I'd legged it down the alleyway.

See, I told you. I'm not brave in the slightest. There's no way I could ever be a guardian angel. Nor a plumber. I mean, how can my dad spend his life sticking his hand down other people's pipes?

I shuddered again at the thought of the fish eyes. My head was reeling, my legs were shaking. My life was suddenly starting to look like some low-budget horror movie. Complete with supernatural ghostie (the hoodie-angel), blood and guts (fish eyes and feet, for goodness' sake), and a potential murderous pie slasher (Thelma Potts). And somehow right in the middle of it all was me, except no one had bothered to give me the script.

Fish-eye pie? I shook my head and trudged off to the cafe at the end of the street.

'Three teas and a packet of smoky bacon crisps, please,' I said.

The cafe was full of people, which felt quite reassuring – as though normal life still existed away from the madness of my day.

'Do you want milk in the tea, love?'

The lady behind the counter was smiling and I felt my spirits lift. But it didn't last, because all of a sudden I felt a giant poke in my back.

'Hey, Lavender Rise! What do you think you're doing?'

I gulped. I instantly knew it was him. (Though actually, he didn't smell quite so bad this time, not compared to the pie shop.)

'What do you want?' I squeaked, looking around to see if everyone was staring. (Though, strangely, no one seemed in the slightest bit concerned to have a six-foot angel in the shop.)

'Why aren't you saving Thelma Potts?' the hoodie-angel barked.

I turned around. He still hadn't sorted out his brightness setting.

'She doesn't need saving,' I snapped, shielding my eyes. 'I was trying to tell you last night. She's ten times stronger than me…'

The hoodie-angel rolled his eyes and folded his arms.

'…And she has four big brothers, and no end of kitchen weaponry. If she's got a problem, trust me, she can sort it out herself.'

The hoodie-angel scowled, but said nothing. So I tried again. 'You see, I want to be a footballer not an angel. Honestly, I make a rubbish angel. I'm much better at kicking a ball than saving people.' The hoodie's scowl deepened. 'But if you lot really want me to spend my time helping people,' I gabbled, 'then maybe I can find someone more deserving. Like some little old lady who needs her grass cutting…'

The hoodie-angel's face turned red and he started counting. When he got to ten, he took a deep breath. 'Look, pal, you'd better sharpen up your act or you'll be in big trouble! Thelma Potts is in serious danger. And time is running out. Tomorrow you must stay close to her, or something very bad will happen. And if it does, you'll be in serious trouble yourself. So stop supping tea and get out there and save her. Or else!'

When he said 'or else', it echoed like we were in a big dark cave, and I was sure I felt the ground shake.

'That'll be £2.50 please, love.'

'What?'

The lady behind the counter was holding out a bag. 'Three teas and a packet of smoky bacon crisps…'

When I turned back, the hoodie-angel had gone.

chapter 7

I dropped some coins on the counter, grabbed the bag and dashed out of the shop.

I wanted to run away, find somewhere without hoodie-angels, plumbing problems, fish-eye pies or Thelma Potts.

And then I spotted it.

Across the road from the café. A shop I'd never noticed before, which wasn't surprising, because it wasn't really my sort of a place. Or yours, either. Trust me.

It was a pink shop with 'Heaven Sent' written in loopy writing. And a window display full of pink and silver nick-nacks. But, of course, that's not what made me cross the road and walk straight in. It was the big pink sign in the window: 'Understand your inner angel. Free readings – help and advice given'.

I know, I know. I wasn't battling with an inner angel. Mine was definitely an outer angel, and it was currently hounding me night and day.

But where else could I go? The local cop shop? Yeah, right! 'Excuse me officer, there's a six-foot angel bothering me…' They'd lock me up in a nut house.

As I walked in, a dainty bell tinkled above my head and I was smothered in a cloud of sugary perfume, while my feet sank into a deep-pile, pink carpet. It felt a bit like visiting my auntie Ada's house. (She's the type of woman who puts fluffy-skirted dollies over her toilet rolls and has crocheted cushions on her sofa.)

I sighed. It felt strangely comforting.

'Are you looking for anything in particular?'

The voice belonged to a small, black-haired head that appeared from behind a big counter at the back of the shop.

'Er… well,' I stammered.

'Looking for a present for your mum's birthday?' asked the head.

'No!' She clearly didn't know my mum. For her last birthday she asked for new overalls: mud brown, with built-in tool belt and extra padding on the knees for especially hard plumbing jobs.

'Your gran then?' the head was obviously keen to nail a sale. 'We've got some lovely potpourri? Or how about an angelic ornament?'

I glanced at a wall covered in horrendous ceramic angels and shuddered.

'No angels!' I said firmly.

The head looked a bit confused, as though I'd walked into a butcher's shop and said I didn't want to buy any meat.

'Actually, I wanted to find out more about the, er… sign outside.'

The head peered at me. 'You mean you want an angel reading?' It looked shocked.

I didn't know what an angel reading was, but it didn't sound very appealing. 'I'm not sure,' I said.

Then the head disappeared below the counter, and a few seconds later reappeared under a hatch along with its body.

'It's not me that does the readings.'

Thank God for that. She was about my age, and dressed head to pointy toes in black leather. She looked like she would be much better equipped to give a full and frank guide to hell, rather than heaven.

'It's my aunt,' she smiled. 'But she's in with someone right now.' She nodded to a pink door at the back, and I noticed her green nose stud glittered when she moved.

'Take a seat on the sofa and she'll be right with you.'

I suddenly felt a bit silly, plus I still had the tea to deliver. I was about to turn tail and head back to the pie shop, when I suddenly got that weird feeling again, like someone nipping my ears. I looked around, in case the hoodie-angel had somehow snuck in from somewhere. But no...

Just then the pink door opened and two women appeared. I knew instantly which one was the aunt, because she actually looked like the angel that sat on our Christmas tree. Right down to the blonde, curly hair and gossamer skirt. She was shaking hands with the other woman, who seemed extremely delighted with her reading.

49

I turned to go, as quickly as I could without actually running, but she'd spotted me.

'Hello, young man… yes… you.' And then she was on me. 'Wait a minute, please, you look troubled.' Her voice was soft and welcoming.

And that's all it took. Two minutes later, I collapsed on her pink, velvet sofa and poured out everything that had happened in my life so far. Seriously, I went right back to the beginning. I rambled on and on and on…

At some stage the lady had nodded to Goth girl and two mugs of delicious hot chocolate had appeared. (I'd completely forgotten about the takeaway tea that was getting colder by the minute.) And still I went on, spilling out all the stuff about not wanting to Dream the Dream, or be a plumber, how my parents had bought me an enormous tool bag for my birthday when I'd much rather have got a new football kit, how I was being stalked by a thuggy angel, about Thelma Potts and her fish-eye pies, and how I was supposed to stay close to her because something awful was going to happen tomorrow. Then, finally, quite suddenly, I just ran out of words, stopped, and sort of crumpled into a heap.

The angel lady took my hand. I know that probably sounds wet, but it was lovely. She had really soft hands – pink, of course. She placed one on my forehead and I suddenly felt soothed, as though I'd off-loaded all my burdens on to someone else's pink, fluffy shoulders.

'Have you got the feather?' she asked softly.

I had, though I'd no idea why. For some reason I'd tucked it down my right sock before we'd left the house.

She held it lightly in her palm.

'Well, it's genuine,' she said firmly. 'See the golden shimmer…'

I couldn't, to be honest. It looked just like a bog-standard bird feather to me.

But the angel lady was mesmerised. 'I'm afraid this means you must do as your angel says. Though I must say, I'm appalled at his approach.'

'What?' I said, sitting bolt upright, my calm evaporating. 'But I can't really be an angel. And even if by some strange freakish thing I am, how am I supposed to save Thelma Potts, and from what? Honestly, if you knew her, you'd see what I mean. She doesn't need protecting.'

'Sometimes the biggest giants need help from the smallest snails,' the angel lady said with a sigh.

I wasn't altogether sure I liked being called a snail! But I was too polite to say anything.

'I know it's all a bit of a shock,' she said softly. 'But there are angels all around us and not all of them are visitors from heaven. Some are people, just like you and me. Really, it's an honour to be chosen to become someone's guardian angel.'

That didn't make me feel better.

'Maybe Thelma plans to murder her ex-boyfriend tomorrow?' said Goth girl. 'And your mission is to stop her. Sort of save her soul.'

I sighed. That was what I didn't want to hear!

'So you think she wants to poison him with fish-eye pies?'

'I don't think so,' said the girl sternly. 'It sounds more like black magic to me. If you take a closer look at all that stuff that was blocking the pie-shop drain, you'll probably find its newts' feet, fish eyes and pig hair. They're the basic ingredients you need for witchcraft. Personally, I think Thelma's been using the pie-shop kitchen to brew up a potion...'

I couldn't help but laugh. I sat there on the pink sofa, surrounded by angels and had a right good chortle. 'My day just gets better and better,' I grinned through gritted teeth. 'Hocus-pocus pies! I've heard it all now.'

'Perhaps not witchcraft,' said the angel lady soothingly. 'Perhaps the girl is just trying to make a charm to win back her lost love. But whatever it is,' she added. 'I think she's in trouble, and for some reason you're the only one who can help her.'

chapter 8

I left soon afterwards. But not before Goth girl had tried to sell me a naff-looking pencil holder, and three packs of cherubic thank-you notes she said were on special offer.

'My aunt needs the cash,' she said grumpily. 'She spends so much time helping people, she forgets to sell anything.'

Guiltily, I bought a pink pencil sharpener with a love heart on it and vowed to throw it away the minute I got out of the shop. I also left with two bits of advice from the angel lady. Firstly, and most importantly, she told me not to worry about wings. (How did she know I was worried? She was right of course: I was absolutely brown-pants panicking that I was about to sprout a huge pair of feathered appendages that I'd somehow have to hide at football practice.)

She also told me to listen to my inner angel. That bit of advice didn't sound useful at all.

Because so far my inner angel was telling me I should go home and hide under my bed for three weeks. But I thanked her anyway, and promised to give her an update soon.

By the time I got back to the pie shop, Dad and Grant had finished and were now sitting scoffing pies in the slightly less smelly pie-shop kitchen.

'At last!' said Dad, dribbling pie fat down his chin.

'I er… bumped into a friend,' I said lamely, offering them cups of stone-cold tea.

Dad smiled. 'Ah, don't fret, son, I know what we found today wasn't pleasant. Sometimes plumbing can be tough, but the rewards are immense. You should go and run some water down that sink now – it's like a babbling brook!'

I declined the offer. I also turned down the pie that Grant offered me. I just couldn't forget the fish eyes.

'Grant's been telling me about this pie-eating competition tomorrow,' said Dad, cramming another overloaded forkful into his mouth. 'It's fascinating.' He chewed for several minutes before wiping the grease off his chin. 'Apparently the world record for beef-and-potato, deep-fried pie scoffing stands at 15 pies in ten minutes.'

I gaped. *Fifteen pies in ten minutes*? Impossible! (Almost as impossible as Grant's love for Thelma.)

'That record was actually set back in the 1950s,' said Grant. 'And it's never been broken.'

'That's a lot of pies,' I said.

Grant nodded. 'The record was set by a local man: Stan Spooner – he was known as Mr Pie. He was actually a pie chef here, back when Thelma's Grandpa ran the business….'

I suddenly got that weird feeling again. Like someone was nipping my ears to make sure I was listening. I frowned. It was actually quite annoying.

Grant shook his head sadly. 'A bit of a sad business really. Stan Spooner died the night he set the record.'

'Died?' I breathed. The nipping sensation was getting worse.

'Yes, he somehow managed to swallow all 15 pies, but then he pushed his luck and decided to try for number 16.' Grant sighed. 'It was his undoing. The 16th pie got wedged in his throat and he choked to death.'

'What!' I gasped. 'He died here?'

Grant shrugged his shoulders. 'Competitive eating's a dangerous sport. Not for the faint-hearted. Would you like to see a picture of him?'

Grant beckoned me into the pie shop and there, high above the counter, was a small black-and-white photograph of a cheerful, red-faced bloke holding an enormous pie.

'That's him,' said Grant. 'It was taken just before the competition.'

'What a dreadful way to go,' I whispered. 'Choking on a pie.'

'Oh, it wasn't so bad. Sort of suited him,' said Grant. 'Pies were his life. He always wanted to be famous as a great pie eater, and dying the way he did, well he sort of got his wish. You know he even left his body to medical science. It was in his will. He liked the idea of doctors trying to work out how he could eat so many pies.'

Just then Dad appeared. 'OK, Grant, we'll be off now,' he said. 'Tell Mr Potts I'll let him have my invoice in a day or two.'

I was still too stunned to speak, but my head was swimming with images: Thelma and her pie slice; Charlie Pittam, the love-rat sausage swallower; Stan Spooner choking on pies…

'Hey – I've just had a thought,' beamed Grant. 'Why don't you both come along to the competition tomorrow? You can drop off your bill then, too.'

Dad grinned.

'No!' I tried to shout, but somehow the word wouldn't come out, and I felt the nipping sensation again.

'It'll be a great night. Piles of pies, lots of excitement,' said Grant. 'And I've got a bit of a surprise in store myself.'

Dad beamed. 'We'd be delighted.'

I tried to shout again. 'NO! NO MORE PIES!'

But still nothing came out. And I suddenly had a scary thought: was this my inner angel messing with my mind?

In the car on the way back home, I tried to piece it all altogether. According to the hoodie-angel, something awful was going to happen to Thelma tomorrow. And no matter how much I disliked her (and, more to the point, was terrified of her), I'd been charged with protecting her. Tomorrow was also the night of the pie-eating competition, where her ex-boyfriend would be competing. I knew it was a dangerous sport. People died scoffing pies. People like poor Stan Spooner – the record-breaking pie eater.

Suddenly I had a flash of inspiration. Thelma was obviously going to knobble one of Charlie's pies during the competition. All she needed to do was stick something lumpy in there and hope he'd choke! Fish eyes, newts' feet, a lump of pig hair… they'd all do the trick: no wonder she'd been 'working on some new recipes'. Goth girl had got it wrong. This wasn't anything to do with hocus-pocus high jinks. This was plain and simple murder. And my mission was obviously to somehow stop Thelma from going through with it. But there was one small detail I couldn't quite work out – how was I, William Box, reluctant plumber, and small, skinny eleven-year-old boy, going to stop Thelma from doing *anything*?

chapter 9

'Billy!' bawled Mum. 'It's for you.'

It was the next morning and I was still in my pyjamas when the doorbell rang.

'Who is it?' I yelled. I wasn't expecting anyone. Barry was still on holiday (lucky devil) and all my other friends are never out of bed before twelve.

There was a pause, and then. 'It's Gaby… from the shop!'

Gaby from the shop? What shop? Gaby who? Reluctantly, I decided I'd better find out.

'Hello, Billy, you left your feather behind.'

It was Goth girl.

'Oh, right,' I muttered. I could see Mum hovering in the kitchen with a smile on her face. My heart sank. She obviously thought that this was my girlfriend. 'Well, thanks for dropping it off. Be seeing you…'

I tried to shut the door, but her small, black leather boot was blocking the way.

'So, Billy,' she said cheerfully, 'have you worked out how you're going to stop Thelma from slicing up that sausage swallower?'

'Ssh!' I said. 'Keep it down.' I could see Mum craning her neck from the kitchen, with that same soppy look on her chops. Actually I *had* finally worked out a plan. 'It's simple,' I said confidently. 'I'm going to go back to the pie shop and tell Thelma I'm there to do a follow-up examination of the plumbing system. That way I'll be able to keep my eye on her and find out what she's really up to.'

'Well, that's rubbish,' said Gaby. 'For a start, Thelma's not working today. I've just been to the shop, looking for you. Grant the pie chef gave me your dad's card. That's how I got here.'

'Great! Well, thanks again for the feather. Be seeing you.'

I tried to shut the door again, but still she wouldn't move her boot.

'Thelma's at home,' she went on. 'Grant told me. And I checked the phone book, so now I know where she lives...'

She was beginning to sound like one of those scary stalkers you read about.

'Fantastic,' I said sarcastically. 'Well, as soon as I've had my shower, I'll go round there and tell her I'm her guardian angel, ready to save the day – and stop her killing her ex-boyfriend.'

Gaby scowled. 'You can't do that!' she snapped. 'But maybe we could go round there together and sort of keep a lookout. Make sure she isn't up to anything.'

'*We?*' I said.

'Well, two of us won't look so suspicious. No offence, Billy, but if I saw you hanging around outside my house, I think I'd call someone.'

She sort of had a point. I sighed. I wished I had an excuse not to go. But I didn't. Dad had been called out on an emergency plumbing job in the early hours and was now snoozing it off. I was surplus to requirements.

'I suppose you'd better come in,' I said.

While I got dressed, Gaby scribbled her aunt's number on a piece of (pink) paper, which I gave to my mum, along with a cock-and-bull story about going around to Gaby's with a gang of kids from school to watch a DVD.

Mum smirked a strange smirk that I hadn't seen before. And, annoyingly, I felt my face turn red. I grabbed my coat and escaped.

'Have you got your tool bag?' asked Gaby.

'Why?'

'Because it might come in handy – you know, a cover for why we might be in Thelma's neighbourhood. You could pretend you're doing a plumbing job.'

I stared at her. My tool bag weighed a ton. There was no way I wanted to lug it around. But then again, I might actually feel safer around Thelma if I had several heavy tools within reach. A few moments later, I reappeared with my bag. And we were off.

Gaby was smaller than me (which is saying something), but she was much faster. It was like going for a walk with a whippet. She powered alongside me, every so often getting so far ahead she'd have to stop and wait. It was actually quite annoying. Then, suddenly, she stopped.

'This is it,' she said, peering at a bit of (pink) paper. 'Number four – the big house over there.'

There's obviously a lot of dosh in pies, because we'd arrived at a pretty posh neighbourhood. The cars were all shiny and new, and the gardens were stuffed full of those adventure play centres that only truly rich kids own. Some of them were bigger than my house.

'Let's take a closer look,' whispered Gaby. She grabbed my arm and we went towards the house.

But a moment later, she suddenly shoved me sideways, really hard. (For someone so small she had iron-man arms.) We landed in a thorny bush.

'OWWWWWWWWWW!' I screamed, or I would have done, if Gaby hadn't clamped her small, sweaty hand over my mouth.

'I think she's coming,' she whispered.

I wriggled a bit. It was hard not to with a giant thorn stuck in my behind.

Gaby pinched my arm. 'Ssh!'

And then I saw her. It was Thelma all right. She was walking briskly down the road, pulling one of those old-lady shopping trolleys behind her, and she had a determined look on her face.

chapter 10

I felt my heart pounding, and I wondered whether it was from fear of Thelma, or the fact that I was struggling to breathe with Gaby's hand over my face.

A few moments later, Gaby let go, and I collapsed back onto the pavement.

'Don't ever do that again!' I yowled.

But Gaby wasn't listening. 'Come on, she's getting on that bus.'

Thelma had reached the end of the street, and as if by magic, a bus had just appeared.

'We can't follow her,' I gasped, as Gaby dragged me towards the bus stop. 'She'll recognise me.'

'Maybe not.' Gaby fumbled in the pocket of her leather trench coat. 'Here put this on.'

'I'm not wearing that!'

It was disgusting. Like a robber's balaclava. The type of thing the thugs wear on *Crimewatch*. And as disguises go it was pants, especially as I was carrying a bag full of tools.

'I might as well hang a sign around my neck saying: Look at me, I'm on my way to rob your house,' I muttered.

But Gaby wasn't listening. She just snatched the balaclava from me, and pulled it down over my face.

'Two fares to town, please.'

And that was that. She shoved me up the middle of the bus past Thelma, who was so busy reading a book, she didn't even glance our way.

'Macaverty and Lawson!' whispered Gaby, as the bus moved off. 'I knew it.'

'What are you talking about?' I pulled off the balaclava and sank into my seat.

'She's reading a really outdated witchcraft manual. She's not even got the revised edition. Personally, I wouldn't use it as bog paper.'

I sighed. 'Look, is there something you want to tell me, Gaby, because I really don't like all this hocus-pocus wizardy stuff. It's just not my bag. Are you a witch?'

Gaby pouted. 'Of course not. I'm just extremely well-read.'

She folded her arms and went into a sulk. But it didn't last long because just then Thelma stood up and rang the bell. Seconds later, the bus stopped and she and her trolley hurried away.

'Come on!' Gaby yelled.

Then we leapt off the bus and chased after her.

Thelma was heading for the hospital.

'Well, that's one place we can't follow,' I said, cheerfully. 'We can't exactly stalk her while she visits her sick granny.'

'She isn't going in,' whispered Gaby.

She wasn't. Thelma walked straight past the hospital entrance and round the corner, where a sign was pointing to the medical school.

We followed at a distance, trying not to look too conspicuous (which was almost impossible, what with me struggling with my giant tool bag that clanked and rattled every time I moved). But, miraculously, she didn't notice us.

'She's not going to the medical school, either,' said Gaby.

She wasn't. Thelma walked past the main medical school building, took a side path and then disappeared through a black doorway.

'Hell's bells,' breathed Gaby, pointing to a sign:

ANATOMY LIBRARY
MEDICAL STUDENTS ONLY

'What is it?' I asked, somehow not quite wanting to know the answer.

Gaby gasped. 'That's where they keep all the pickled people!'

'What do you mean pickled people?' I literally downed tools. My bag landed heavily on my toes but I didn't care. I just couldn't lug the thing any further.

Gaby rolled her eyes. 'An anatomy library is where they keep specimens – you know like feet and hands and skeletons… It's where medical students learn about how the body works! Don't they teach you anything at school?'

I scowled. 'And what school do you go to – Winnie the Witch comprehensive?'

'I'm home-educated, actually,' she spat back.

We glared at each other, and then Gaby shrugged. 'Look, now is not the time to fall out. We've got to get in there and see what Thelma's doing.'

I shook my head. 'Whatever she's doing in there, I don't want to know.'

As soon as I'd said it, I felt a nipping around my ears again. I jiggled uncomfortably on the spot.

Gaby shot me a look that seemed to say: you

are the oddest boy I've ever come across. Then she sighed. 'Well, I'm going in.'

And that's when I got cross. I don't know whether it was the nipping around my ears, the exhaustion from lugging my tool bag, or just Gaby's grumpy face, but suddenly I reached the end of my fuse. And I sort of exploded.

'Look! Wait one minute. If anyone is going in there, it's me!' (The nipping suddenly stopped.) 'I mean, this is my story. I'm the angel here – OK?'

Gaby froze. Her face turned pink and she looked like she was about to say something, but then thought better of it.

'You're right,' she mumbled. 'So, come on then. What are we waiting for?'

'Exactly,' I agreed.

I hauled up my tool bag and we headed for the door.

Despite my bravado, I was quaking in my steel toe caps (regulation plumber's wear).

'What's that smell?' I gasped, as we pushed through the first set of double doors.

'Formaldehyde,' whispered Gaby. 'It's the pickle juice.'

Through the second set of doors, the smell

got worse. We were now standing in a corridor in front of another set of double doors. Above was a sign:

SPECIMENS MUST NOT BE REMOVED

Underneath was a smaller sign:

The Anatomy Library is open between 3pm and 7pm for assistance outside these hours, please call the main medical school library on ext 4224 to obtain a key.

I checked my watch. It was only 11.30.

'It should be locked,' I whispered.

Gaby gave the door a push. 'Well, Thelma must have found the key.'

With a pounding heart, we crept inside. I half expected Thelma to be waiting, pie slice in hand, ready to pop me straight into a pickle jar. But she wasn't anywhere to be seen. In fact, there was no one there at all, at least no one alive…

chapter 11

At first it just looked like a storeroom: there were wooden shelves, benches, filing cabinets. And then I looked more closely, and realised what was on the shelves – rows and rows of jars. A bit like the big ones you get in the chip shop. You know, with pickled onions and beetroot in them. But there were no onions or beetroot in these jars. There were feet and hands, fingers and ears… and bits I didn't recognise at all.

I shuddered, but it was strangely fascinating. Even to a big scaredy-cat like me, and I couldn't tear my eyes away.

'I'll go through to the next room,' whispered Gaby, 'and see if I can spot Thelma. You keep watch.'

I nodded. But I didn't really register what she said. I just stood there, slack-jawed, peering at the various parts of people in the jars. One particular pot caught my attention. It contained an eye. I gasped. There's something about a sightless eye, with its raggedy edges, and milky-white surround, peering back at you from a small glass jar. My stomach lurched. Visions of bloodied fish eyes suddenly filled my brain. I felt another heave, and looked around desperately for something to barf into, but all I could find was my tool bag. Dad would disown me. I just couldn't do it. So I clamped my hand over my mouth and tried to swallow instead.

And then Gaby appeared.

I coughed and shuffled my feet. The last thing in the world I wanted was for her to see how green I was feeling. I'd never hear the end of it. But luckily she didn't notice.

'Come on!' she shrieked, pulling me away from all the jars. 'Thelma's coming!'

We ran back through the doors and out along the path, ducking behind a large tree just in time to see Thelma walking briskly past, pulling her shopping trolley behind her. I noticed with a shiver that the trolley was obviously heavier than before, as she was using two hands. And what was that big bulge down one side?

'Bones!' whispered Gaby. 'A whole trolley-load of them.'

'What?' I gasped.

'She pinched a skeleton. I saw her do it. She just opened one of the cases, pulled out a skeleton, and stuffed all the bits in her trolley.'

'What does she want a skeleton for?'

Gaby frowned. 'It's all pointing to a zombie spell, if you ask me.'

'A what?'

'You know – bringing a body back to life. She's got all the ingredients: fish eyes, pigs' hair, newts' feet, and a big bag of bones…'

I laughed. 'Don't be ridiculous! What would Thelma want with a zombie?'

'Maybe she doesn't want to get her hands dirty,' said Gaby. 'If she's planning to kill this ex-boyfriend of hers – what's he called, Charlie Pittam? – well, it would be much easier to get a zombie to do it…'

'That's just bonkers,' I gasped. 'People don't go around getting zombies to murder their ex-boyfriends.'

'Nor do they get visited by scary-looking angels in the middle of the night.' Gaby folded her arms and put her nose in the air.

She had a point. The world had gone mad. And one further step into la-la land, seemed quite reasonable.

I shrugged. 'Just supposing what you say is true. How can we stop her?'

'Well, it might help if we know whose skeleton she's just pinched. If he was a murderer or something, we would know what we're up against.'

'A *murderer*?' I gasped.

'Oh, yes – in the olden days, murderers' bodies were often handed over to medical students, you know, after they'd been hung…'

My throat suddenly started to tingle, and I was having trouble breathing.

'All we need to do is look up his name,' she said cheerfully. 'There must be a records office in the medical school. They'll be able to tell us what he was hung for.'

'But we haven't got a name,' I grumbled.

'Yes, we have,' said Gaby smugly. 'It was written on the glass case. I could see it clearly – Stan Spooner – which doesn't sound much like a killer to me…'

'Stan Spooner!' I gasped. 'It can't be.'

My heart started to race, and I felt that annoying nipping sensation again – except now it was even more intense. 'That's the name of the champion pie eater who choked to death at Potts' Pies in 1956.'

'How do you know that?' said Gaby.

'Oh, you know,' I said shakily. 'I'm just extremely well-read.' I stood up. 'Come on, I'll tell you everything on the way home.'

'Home?' Gaby shook her head. 'We can't go home, Billy. Don't you see what this means?'

'No.' I definitely did not.

'If this Stan Spooner guy is some sort of competitive eater – and tonight's the night of the big pie-eating competition, then there must be a link. Thelma's clearly planning to turn Stan into a zombie and get him to bump off her ex-boyfriend at tonight's competition. Come on. We've got to stop her!' Gaby grabbed my arm. 'We'll take the bus,' she said firmly. 'And we'll still beat Thelma home. Trust me, she'll be walking. She won't want to risk someone taking a close look at that shopping trolley.'

I lugged my tool bag back to the bus stop and wished that I had just Dreamed the stupid Dream. Plumbing had to be easier than all this do-gooding.

chapter 12

Once again, Gaby was right. When we got back to Thelma's street there was no sign of her. I checked my watch. Four o'clock.

'Two hours to go before the pie-eating competition,' I said.

'Two hours to stop Thelma,' said Gaby.

We climbed over her garden wall, me still with my big tool bag, and Gaby trying not to get mud on her boots. Then we took up position behind the compost heap. The fact that it stank and was covered in slugs and worms didn't bother me. I was getting used to disgusting stuff.

And then Thelma appeared, dragging the trolley with her. She didn't even glance at the house, she just headed for the shed. When I say shed, you're probably thinking small wooden hut for keeping your lawn mower in. But you'd be wrong. This shed looked like a Swiss chalet – you know, the type of place Heidi lived in.

It was enormous, with fancy, fluted windows and a porch. I even found myself wondering whether it had its own loo. (Mental note: must stop thinking plumber-type thoughts: personally I blamed the bag – it seemed to be infecting me.) Anyway, Thelma and the trolley disappeared inside.

'Let's go and look in the window,' whispered Gaby.

But before we could move, Thelma shut the curtains.

'Bother!' snapped Gaby. 'How are we going to find out what she's doing now?'

'Maybe we should just go home?' I said hopefully.

Gaby scowled at me. 'You're such a wimp.'

'Me?' I was taken aback – I thought I'd been pretty brave, all things considered. I suddenly felt cross. 'Oh, shut up! Why don't you get back on your broomstick and buzz off.'

'No, you buzz off,' snapped Gaby.

'All right then, I will,' I hadn't meant to say it, but now I had, I sort of had to carry it through. So I stood up, wiped the mud off my jeans and stalked off. Really, Gaby was the most infuriating girl I'd ever had the misfortune to meet. And if she wanted to spend her evening spying on Thelma Potts then that was her lookout. Personally, I was quite glad to be rid of them both. And my heart lifted at the thought that yes, I could actually just go home…

I was halfway over the wall when I suddenly felt a hand on my ankle.

'Get off, Gaby!' I growled.

But it wasn't Gaby.

'Hey, plumber boy. Where do you think you're going?'

I looked back, and was immediately blinded by the bright, white light.

'I… er… well…' Actually, I didn't have an answer.

The hoodie-angel hauled me back into the garden. And I landed with a bump in a particularly nasty bramble bush.

'That hurt!' I howled.

'It was meant to,' the hoodie-angel sneered. 'Now, what do you think you're doing legging it when Thelma is on the edge of oblivion?'

What a drama queen! I plucked a thorn out of my thigh and tried not to get cross.

'Look,' I said, smiling as politely as I could. 'Whatever Thelma's up to, there's nothing I can

79

do to stop her.' I shrugged. 'It may have escaped your notice, but I am not Spiderman. Or Superman. Or any other bloke in silly tights you might have muddled me up with. I'm an eleven-year-old schoolboy…'

The hoodie-angel scowled. 'Well, if you want to stay being an eleven-year-old schoolboy, you'd better start following orders – otherwise you'll be looking at a trip upstairs, permanently!' He pointed skywards and had an exceedingly menacing look on his face.

'What?' I gasped. 'But I don't want to go to Heaven. Not yet. I've got sinks to unblock, toilets to fix…' (*What*? What was I blethering about? I was completely losing it. I definitely had to ditch the tool bag at the earliest opportunity.)

The hoodie-angel was unmoved. 'Well, you should have thought about that before you signed the contract…' He fished inside his pocket and withdrew a crumbled bit of white paper. 'Look, it says here quite clearly: "Failure to comply with direct Heavenly orders will result in an Earthbound angel being reassigned to other duties, elsewhere, permanently".'

'But you didn't tell me that,' I squeaked.

'You should always read the small print,' he chuckled. 'Now, are you going to get in that shed and sort out Thelma Potts, or do I need to get heavy?'

I didn't really have much choice. I was caught between the wrath of Heaven and a zombie-making pie slasher. What would you have done?

I gathered up my tool bag and legged it to the other side of the garden, where Gaby was still hiding behind the compost heap totally oblivious to the menacing I'd just received from the feathered freak.

And that's when Thelma spotted me.

'WHAT DO YOU THINK YOU'RE DOING?'

I had almost reached the compost heap when she appeared at the shed door with a bucket and shovel in her hands.

I froze.

She looked like she was about to dig my grave.

'YOU'RE TRESPASSING!' she yelled, and then suddenly she realised who I was. 'YOU!' she gasped. 'IT'S YOU AGAIN!'

And then she flew at me, swinging the shovel wildly around her head. She looked like a runaway helicopter with lethal chopper blades and a mad pilot. I shut my eyes and prepared for the end.

'Don't touch him!' yelled Gaby, emerging from behind the compost heap. 'He can't help it if he's madly in love with you.'

'What?' Even in my state of abject terror, I still couldn't miss what she'd said.

'*What?*' Even Thelma was shocked. 'And who are you, anyway?'

'Gaby,' said Gaby. 'A friend of Billy's.' (What a liar!) 'He's too shy to tell you himself, so he asked me to come along and speak for him. Look, he's even bought you a present.'

Gaby fished inside my coat pocket and pulled out the love-heart pencil sharpener she'd made me buy from her aunt's shop. (She'd obviously seen me stash it away before I left the shop. I could have kicked myself for keeping it.)

I tried to explain, but my mouth wouldn't work.

Thelma's eyes narrowed, as though she suspected a setup. 'But he's just a kid,' she growled.

'He may be a kid, but he'd do anything for you,' said Gaby. 'Truly, *anything*.'

I didn't like the sound of that. Gradually I seemed to be regaining the power of speech – like a frozen leg of lamb that's started to thaw – but my tongue still didn't seem to fit in my mouth properly. I tried to deny all Gaby's rubbish, but my words just sort of came out in a slur.

'See?' said Gaby. 'That's the effect you have on him.'

Thelma put down her shovel, and suddenly clocked my tool bag.

'Have you got any screwdrivers in there?'

I nodded dumbly. I had 28 screwdrivers – enough screwdrivers to fit any head, anywhere.

This news seemed to soften her slightly.

'Well, I need to borrow one. But neither of you can breathe a word of this. If you do, I'll flatten you!'

And with that, we entered Thelma's world.

chapter 13

Thelma closed the door and – my heart sank – locked it.

'Now, listen,' she growled, standing in front of the door with her arms folded. 'I'm involved in a bit of an… um… experiment. It's a science project for school.'

I was happy to play along with the 'science project' story, but Gaby wasn't.

She immediately pointed at a big book propped up on the table. 'If I'm not very much mistaken, that's Macaverty and Lawson – a first edition, and I believe you're about to do some practical magic.'

I could have kicked her. As approaches go, that was even less subtle than my hoodie-angel's.

'What?' Thelma gasped. 'I don't know what you're talking about.'

Gaby smiled, a smug smile…

'Don't worry, we won't tell, I'm a bit of a dabbler myself, if I'm honest.'

I knew it! I knew it! All that black eyeliner. And those silly, pointy boots. She probably has a broom down her back and a black cat in her handbag. Witches, I hate 'em!

Thelma was flummoxed, which was actually quite satisfying to see.

'If you want, I can help you,' said Gaby. 'I suspect you were on your way out to the compost heap to find worms.'

Thelma nodded uncertainly.

'Well, how about I get the worms while Billy here wires up the skeleton – because I'm guessing that's what you had in mind for his screwdrivers.'

'Yes,' whispered Thelma. 'It needs to be put back together – it's in a bit of a mess…'

I gulped. I was pretty sure this wasn't what the hoodie-angel had in mind when he'd told me I had to help Thelma.

'Only a couple of other things we need,' said Gaby cheerfully. 'Have you got the base stock?'

The what?

Gaby glanced at me and saw the bewilderment on my face. 'Every spell needs a base. For this one, I think I'm right in saying that you squish 600 fish eyes through a strainer, then simmer the liquid with newts' feet, and finally wrap it all up in pigs' hair, and roast for three hours.

Thelma's mouth opened, but no words came out. Instead, she reached into a basket on the table and took out a plastic tub.

Gaby smiled. 'Good. The only other thing you need for a zombie spell is a tempter.'

'A what?' Again I was lost.

'Something to tempt the dead back to life.'

Thelma rummaged in the basket again, and produced a huge pie.

'Perfect.' said Gabby. 'I'm sure our zombie won't be able to resist.'

It was completely bonkers. But suddenly we were all very busy.

Thelma upended the trolley and Stan Spooner tumbled to the floor. I picked up his skull. Strangely, I didn't feel funny. It was like I was part of a play, and I was just acting the role of wizardy odd-job man.

I had a good look at the screws that had been drilled into the bottom of the skull. 'I think I have a screwdriver that'll do the job,' I muttered.

Of course I did. My tool bag could probably have done the job for me.

'Well, make sure you wire him up properly,' snapped Thelma, who was swiftly getting back to her old self. 'I don't want any mess ups.'

'What exactly are you planning to do with Mr Spooner?' asked Gaby, who'd returned with her bucket of worms.

'How do you know who he is?' said Thelma, all suspicious again.

'My cousin is a medical student,' said Gaby confidently. 'And a few months ago, he gave me a tour of the anatomy library. I remember Mr Spooner's distinctively large jaw bone.'

It was clearly a total fib. But Thelma bought it.

'Also,' went on Gaby, 'when you produced that pie there, as the "tempter", I knew I was right. A pie for Mr Pie,' she giggled.

Gaby was the oddest girl I'd ever met. After a bit, she stopped giggling and cocked her head to one side. 'But one thing I'm intrigued to know is how you managed to get into the anatomy library to steal Stan. As I remember, it's usually locked up.'

Thelma smirked. 'The hospital janitor is one of our best customers. You'd be amazed at how helpful people can be when you offer them free pies. I just told him I wanted to become a doctor, and he was happy to give me a spare set of keys to the library so I could swat up for the medical-school entrance exams.'

Thelma looked at us closely for a moment, and then seemed to make a decision.

'I suppose I should tell you what I'm planning, but I meant what I said earlier; if either of you breathe a word, I'll mince you!'

'Cross my heart,' said Gaby smiling.

'Er... me, too,' I muttered, as I scrabbled about in my tool bag (secretly wishing it would swallow me up).

Thelma sighed. 'I need Stan Spooner to teach someone a lesson.'

Here we go, I thought. You need Stan Spooner to stick a pie cleaver into your ex-boyfriend's head.

'There's a man I know called Charlie Pittam.' Thelma's lips tightened and she puffed up her enormous chest. 'He made a fool out of me. Told me he loved me, when all along he just wanted free pies so he could get in training for tonight's pie-eating competition.'

Gaby nodded sympathetically, as though she'd had similar experiences.

'Well, I decided that the only way to really get back at Charlie was to stop him from winning the competition.'

'What?' I looked up. 'You mean you're not planning to kill him?'

Thelma frowned, and then ignored me. 'Charlie's a dead cert to win tonight. He's going to go for the pie record. Sixteen pies in ten minutes. And he'll do it – I've seen him eat 17 in a practice session. But there's one man who can match him.' She pointed at the pile of bones.

'But he's dead,' I said. 'Dead men don't win pie-eating competitions.'

'They will tonight,' snapped Thelma. 'He has to!'

Just then there was a crack of thunder from outside, and suddenly the sky opened up. Rain lashed against the window pane.

'How appropriate,' I sighed.

chapter 14

Wiring a skeleton is not easy. Have you ever tried? Honestly, it's impossible. There are so many fiddly bits. But I was doing my best while Thelma and Gaby poured over their recipe book.

You know that old phrase about 'too many cooks', well, I was starting to see the point. There they were, both squabbling over everything: who should say what; who should hold the pie… I was quite glad to be left alone with Stan. Though I was becoming increasingly worried that I seemed to have too many screws left over. I decided they must just be spares.

'Are you done yet?' growled Thelma. (That was her being friendly.)

Seeing as Thelma wasn't actually planning to kill her ex-boyfriend, I'd decided it was probably OK for me to help her make her zombie. 'All ready,' I said proudly.

'He looks a bit odd,' said Thelma.

'Yeah, sort of not quite right,' added Gaby.

I frowned. 'Well, he has been dead for 60 odd years.'

I kicked the spare screws out of view.

'Maybe he'll look better in his clothes?' said Gaby, hopefully.

Thelma had brought one of her dad's old suits to dress him in.

Putting clothes on a skeleton is hard work, but once I'd dressed him, he did look much better.

'OK – turn off the lights,' said Gaby.

'Why?' I moaned. I hate the dark.

'Because we need total darkness,' thundered Thelma, who was only just audible over the actual thunder that was still sounding above.

I flicked the switch and shivered. The only light was from the cauldron that the girls had rigged up on the table. (It was actually just a camping stove and an old cooking pan.)

'OK, I think we're ready,' said Gaby. 'Bring Stan forward,' she motioned to me.

Stan was propped up in an old deck chair. I pushed him closer to the table and watched as Thelma picked up one of his long, spindly arms and draped it in the cauldron. In went the pie and then there was silence. (Well, apart from the crazy storm raging outside, which I was beginning to think might be a sign from above that I was letting the side down!)

At last, they started. I've no idea what they said, but it sounded totally ridiculous. Complete hocus-pocus, wizardy bilge. I had to stick my fingers in my mouth to make sure I didn't laugh. (And I was secretly scared of what Thelma might do to me if I spoilt her fun.) But as they went on, I stopped wanting to laugh and began to feel rather uncomfortable. There was something rather unsettling about their rhythm. And then suddenly a scary thought occurred to me – what if this mumbo jumbo really did work? What if we were actually about to bring someone back from the dead?

The room went cold and I heard a rattling noise. I suspected it might be my teeth, which were chattering with cold and fear. But it wasn't.

Stan Spooner's skeleton was shaking.

I bit my lip and prayed that the screws would hold. (As you might have guessed I'm not particularly skilled with a screwdriver – and I didn't like to think what Thelma might do to me if Stan Spooner fell apart.)

The girls started chanting again. And the skeleton started shaking some more. And then the weirdest thing happened: flesh started to appear along his bones.

Honestly. It was truly ghastly. Bubbling blood and flesh pulsated along Stan's bones. I didn't want to look. But just like at the anatomy museum, I couldn't stop myself.

The chanting got louder as the storm grew stronger outside. The window frames were rattling. And Stan was growing more and more human-looking. Hair sprouted on the top of his bony head. Eyes popped into his empty sockets. Then his jaw fell open and I noticed teeth were growing inside.

It was too much. I shut my eyes tight. Then, all of a sudden, there was an almighty crash of thunder, and a streak of lightening lit up the room. I peeked through my fingers, and there, sitting in the deck chair, was the complete Stan Spooner, competitive pie-eating champion. Though he didn't look much like his picture.

'Pies!' he gurgled. 'I want pies!'

Thelma was ecstatic. 'We've done it!' she squealed. 'We've really done it!'

Gaby smiled smugly. 'Of course we have.'

I was speechless.

Thelma put the pie in his hand. And he immediately stuffed it into his mouth. I watched as pie grease ran down his chin.

Thelma clapped her hands in delight.

'He doesn't say much,' I muttered.

'Well, he *is* a zombie,' said Gaby sarcastically. 'They're not known for their powers of conversation.'

'Enough talking,' said Thelma sharply. 'We've got to get him down to the pie shop – the competition starts in less than an hour.'

And that's where the problems began. For some reason, Stan wasn't very steady on his feet.

'He's probably forgotten how to use them,' I said, desperately hoping no one would blame my wiring job.

But every time he tried to stand, his knees gave way and he collapsed again.

'Pies,' he gurgled. 'Pies!' It was all he could say.

'Haul him up!' boomed Thelma. 'I won't let a pair of lousy legs let me down.'

I draped one of his long, bony arms around my shoulders, and Gaby took the other side. I shivered. There's something about touching a zombie. They don't feel very nice. A bit cold and clammy, and slightly soggy, but I was too polite to say anything.

'The wheelbarrow,' said Thelma. 'We'll stick him in there and wheel him to the competition. There's nothing in the rules that say a competitor can't be carried in.'

And that's what we did. We poured him into the wheelbarrow and set off for the shop.

It wasn't easy. Not only did I have to take a turn at pushing Stan, I was also lugging my tool bag. But finally we made it.

We went in the back door, through the kitchen. I was wondering how we'd explain ourselves, but everything was in such chaos that no one noticed. A handful of bakers were running hither and thither, as though they didn't quite know what they were supposed to be doing. There were pies everywhere, stacked up in big, metal serving plates. Stan's eyes were out on stalks, and there was saliva running down his chops. 'Where's Grant?' roared Thelma.

'He hasn't turned up,' squeaked one of the bakers, obviously as terrified of Thelma as the rest of us.

'Where's my dad?' she thundered.

'In the shop – they're introducing the competitors...'

'Quick!' Thelma bellowed to us. 'Grab Stan's arms, and let's get him inside.'

'Pies!' growled Stan.

I shook my head. There was no way we were going to get away with this.

chapter 15

The competitors were lined up at the front of the pie shop, like athletes on a racetrack. I'd expected them all to be enormous. But they weren't.

'Introducing Kelly "the Belly" Bradshaw from Florida, USA.'

There was a round of applause and a few cheers as a skinny woman with a shock of orange hair took a bow.

'And next up we have Gary "the Growler" Gibbons from Adelaide, Australia.'

Another round of applause and a few whoops of delight, as a small man in a khaki boiler suit gave a wave and did a few star jumps.

'And our very own local lad, Charlie "the Pit" Pittam!'

I craned my neck. It was the first time I'd seen the root of all my troubles. He wasn't much to look at. A bit like a mobile-phone salesman: smooth. In fact his face was so smooth it was almost expressionless. (I wondered whether he had some sort of face iron that he used to get the creases out at night.) I noticed he got an extra big cheer from a moon-faced girl in the audience – no doubt she was the sausage heiress.

'And introducing a new competitor, Stanley Smith…'

'That's us!' growled Thelma. 'Come on.'

There was a smattering of polite applause, and a few odd looks, as between us we managed to wrestle Stan into a chair. (I noticed Thelma had taken down Stan's picture from above the counter.)

'And, finally, a late entry, introducing Grant "the Champ" Watkins.'

Thelma did a double take. 'What?!'

It was true. There, taking his seat amongst the other competitors, was Grant the pie chef.

'What's he doing?' squealed Thelma.

Of course I knew, but I was too scared to say. Grant was obviously so besotted with Thelma that he'd decided to reclaim her honour and beat Charlie Pittam at his own game. I shook my head. Grant looked a less-likely competitive pie-eating candidate than I did.

Just then Charlie sauntered over.

'Who's your new friend, Thelma?' he said nastily, looking straight at Stan. 'Aren't you going to introduce us?'

'Pies!' growled Stan.

Thelma blushed scarlet. 'Hello, Charlie,' she said with a wobbly voice. 'I hope you'll be a good loser tonight.'

Charlie swept back his greasy, black hair and sniggered. 'Oh, and he's going to beat me, is he?' He sniggered again, and then went back to his sausage girlfriend.

Well, he had a point. As much as I didn't want to admit it, Stan wasn't looking his best. I'd definitely made a few errors with my rewiring. I'd already noticed he couldn't quite close his jaw properly, and one of his feet had fallen off, but I'd hidden it in my tool bag.

The announcer guy, who looked a bit like Thelma – apart from the bald head and moustache (her dad, I reckoned), picked up his mike again.

'Now, the rules are simple: competitors must not be helped by any of their supporters; they must finish each pie before embarking on their next; they're only allowed to sip water – no other liquids; the time limit is ten minutes and the judges' decision is final. We're pleased to have with us Jeffrey Dullard from *The Guinness Book of Records* to ensure it's a fair and impartial competition. Now, bring on the pies!'

The kitchen doors opened and large silver platters piled high with pies were presented to each competitor, along with a jug of water. Members of Jeffrey Dullard's team were assigned to watch each competitor, and count the pies they consumed.

My heart was racing. This was it. I still wasn't quite sure what I was doing here. I certainly hadn't protected Thelma from her dark side. I'd practically introduced her to it. If it hadn't been for me and my screwdrivers, we wouldn't even be sitting here. I sighed, and started trying to think of ways to explain all this to the hoodie-angel…

chapter 16

'On your marks, get set, GO!'

And we were off. Or rather, Stan was.

Before the start of the contest, he'd been like a greyhound fighting to get out of his trap: Gaby had had to hold his arms down to stop him getting stuck into the pies. So as soon as the whistle went, he grabbed his first pie, and took an enormous bite.

Thelma's grin was as wide as my tool bag.

Stan chomped like crazy, pie fat running down his chin. But the others were getting stuck in, too.

'Kelly the Belly's on pie number two,' whispered Gaby.

But Stan was holding his own. He'd already started on his third, and was at least six mouthfuls ahead of Charlie Pittam.

I wasn't really watching the competition; I was staring at Stan's jaw. There was something not quite right about it. And I suddenly wondered whether I should have made more of an effort to fit the spare screws in somewhere.

'The Growler's on pie number five,' shrieked Thelma. 'Come on, Stan!'

He didn't need much encouragement. Stan increased his pace, and by the time he got to his seventh pie, he was in the lead. But Charlie was hard on his heels.

'Look!' shouted Gaby. 'Grant's on number eight.'

I couldn't really see Grant from where I was sitting. But I didn't bother trying too hard. I knew he was no match for Stan and Charlie.

I was right.

'Stan's on number ten,' roared Thelma.

But so was Charlie…

'Come on, Charlie!' screamed his moon-faced girlfriend. The encouragement worked. Charlie's rhythmic chewing stepped up a beat and within seconds he was on pie number twelve.

I was mesmerised watching him. Round and round he chewed. And then, without missing a beat, he'd take a glug of water, and start another pie. It actually made me feel quite sick.

'THREE MINUTES TO GO!' shouted Thelma's dad.

And that's when disaster struck.

Stan was in the lead on pie 13, when his jaw suddenly stopped. It just froze, like someone had turned off the power.

'Come on, Stan!' boomed Thelma. 'What are you doing?'

But Stan was stuck. Well and truly. His mouth was full of pie, but there was definitely a malfunction somewhere.

I gulped. Now was definitely not the time to own up about the screws.

'Do something, Billy!' thundered Thelma.

But what could I do? The rules were clear. Supporters were not allowed to help. And anyway, by then it was too late.

'Two minutes to go…'

Thelma was close to tears. Stan seemed to have turned grey, and I noticed his bones were starting to show through his skin.

'Gaby!' I gasped. 'What's happening to Stan?'

She shrugged. 'I think the spell might be wearing off. I told you – that first-edition spell book isn't worth bog paper.'

'Come on,' I grabbed her arm. 'I think we'd better get him out of here before he turns back into a bag of bones.'

Together, we manhandled Stan away from the table and to his wheelbarrow in the kitchen. He didn't seem too bothered. In fact he seemed quite relieved. He had a deeply contented smile on his face, as though his belly was full of pie and life felt pretty darn good.

We raced back into the shop just in time to see Kelly the Belly leave the table. She was quitting at pie 13. There were just three of them left: Charlie Pittam, The Australian Growler and, the biggest shocker of all, Grant the pie chef.

'Thirty seconds to go.'

'The Ozzie's out!' gasped Gabby, as the khaki bloke stood up with a face the colour of his shirt.

Charlie and Grant were neck and neck on pie 14. They'd both slowed down considerably. Each mouthful now looked laboured. But astonishingly it was Grant the pie chef who finished first (although he looked sick as a dog). Then, just as Grant reached for his 15th pie, he did a very silly thing. He looked over to Thelma, who was slumped in the corner, and shouted in a very soppy voice, 'Thelma, I love you. This one's for you!' And with that he took an enormous bite.

The audience gasped. Thelma nearly fell off her chair. And Charlie threw up. Literally, and it wasn't a pretty sight, I can tell you.

'Grant, you've won!' squealed Thelma.

The crowd went wild. And Grant went blue. In all the excitement, pie number 15 had got stuck in his throat. At first, everyone was too busy cheering to notice. But then Grant fell under the table and the room went quiet. There were screams and moans and people were queuing up to thump him on the back.

'Call an ambulance!' shouted Thelma's dad.

'He's going to die!' called out Charlie cheerfully.

'Billy!' bawled Thelma. 'Do something!'

Me? Why me? I mean, I'm not exactly a close friend of Thelma's. She can't stand me, for God's sake. But for some reason, it was me she shouted to. And, bizarrely, I responded. I did what any plumber would do – I reached inside my giant tool bag, immediately found my plunger and leapt over the table. I put the plunger carefully over Grant's mouth and nose, and gently plunged three times.

That was all it took. In seconds, I felt movement. I loosened the plunger, and used my finger to winkle out the final piece of pie number 15.

'That's my boy,' came a deep, gravely voice from the door.

It was my dad!

Disaster! The last thing in the world I wanted was for him to see me do anything vaguely connected to a future in plumbing. I could have kicked myself. And then there was uproar. Grant was coughing and puking and thanking me, at the same time as trying to snog Thelma, who was declaring her undying love for him!

Then I was suddenly thrust aloft by the pie-eating fans and flung into the air to a resounding chorus of 'For he's a jolly good fellow…'

What a night.

Or should that be night*mare*?

Eventually, things calmed down. Grant was crowned pie-eating champ of the night, though as he hadn't actually finished his final pie (which had very nearly finished him off), Stan's record was declared safe, which I felt quite glad about. Thelma's dad promised me a lifetime's supply of free pies. (He'd secretly admitted that his pie shop couldn't take another death on the premises. Personally I think they should scrap the competition, it's too dangerous.) Thelma and Grant asked me to be their best man, when they tie the knot in five years' time. (They really did set the date and everything.) Thelma also took me aside and said she was touched that I loved her, and that I'd saved Grant's life, but I could never be more than a brother to her – for which I thank my lucky stars. Charlie Pittam left with his new girlfriend, muttering about how pies were overrated, and sausages were much more his thing. And my dad toured the room, telling anyone he could corner long enough that I was a real chip off the old block and he was planning to enter me in the plunging event of the next Olympics. (Don't laugh. It's true. They do actually hold a plumbing Olympics every four years. You see what sort of life I have to look forward to?) Gaby, who'd disappeared for a while, returned to tell me that she'd wheeled Stan into the back alley behind the shop. He was unfortunately now a bag of bones again, but Gaby said he'd had the happiest smile she'd ever seen on a skeleton. (And, of course, she's seen hundreds.) We both agreed to meet up the next day to somehow return Stan to his box in the anatomy library. And me? I was just glad to go home.

chapter 17

'Hey, Lavender Rise, what's with the beauty sleep?'

I actually smelt him before I saw him. It was eleven o'clock and I wasn't asleep. I was waiting for him. I wanted him to tell me it was all over. And that I didn't have to watch over Thelma for the rest of my life…

'Well, you didn't exactly save Thelma from her dark side, did you?' he scolded.

I sighed. I knew I was probably in the heavenly doghouse.

Then the hoodie-angel grinned. 'But they're pleased with you anyway. By doing such a dreadful job with those screws, the zombie thing was never going to work. And, most importantly, you saved Grant, so Thelma will live happily ever after.'

I suddenly felt weary. 'All I want to know is whether I'm finished. Can I stop taking care of Thelma now?'

He nodded. 'That mission is over.'

'And what about the ear nipping? I presume that was all your doing?'

The hoodie-angel smirked. 'Not guilty. Blame yourself for that one. As soon as you signed the guardian-angel contract, your inner angel was unleashed. All that ear stuff was your inner angel making sure you were paying attention to the important stuff.'

I gasped. My life couldn't get much worse. An ugly looking outer angel hounding me day and night was one thing, but having to deal with an ear-pinching, do-gooding inner angel as well, was quite another.

'And I'll tell you something else to cheer you up,' the hoodie-angel laughed.

I sighed. Now I was free of Thelma, I just wished he'd push off.

'You know, the truth is you weren't supposed to do this.'

'*What?*' I sat up. 'What do you mean?'

'I mean I got it a bit wrong.' The hoodie-angel grinned an even bigger grin (quite a menacing sight, I can tell you). 'There are two William Boxes in this house, right? Well, we wanted the other one, not you.'

'My *dad*?' I breathed. It made complete sense. My dad really was a time-served hero.

'Yeah, but the good news is, they reckon you've done such a good job that you deserve the gig.'

'What!' I yelped.

'Yep – you've earned your wings.'

'But I don't want my wings. I don't want to be an angel!'

'Tough,' growled the hoodie-angel, suddenly looking grumpy again. 'Some people are never satisfied.'

I leapt out of bed and prodded his chest. 'Now, listen here. I do not want to be an angel, not now, not ever.'

He was so taken aback that someone so small and puny would dare to prod him, that he laughed; a big nasty belly laugh, and gave me a wink. 'You're really something else. Anyway, must fly now, but I'll be seeing you again soon.' And with that he disappeared into the wardrobe.

I ran after him. But this time, he didn't leave so much as a feather.

I collapsed on my bed and felt like weeping. But then I changed my mind. Tears were for wimps. What I needed was action. I pulled off my pyjamas and got into my plumbing overalls. I opened my tool bag and took out my tool belt. I filled it with every plumbing tool that would fit and squashed the rest down my socks and under my overall. It wasn't very comfy, I can tell you. Then I found every plumbing book I own and stuck them all over my bed. Finally, I carefully climbed under the covers.

If this lot didn't make me Dream the Dream, then nothing would. After all, I am William Box – I come from a long line of trusted and respected plumbers. I am not, nor will I ever be an angel. It's just not my destiny.

The End (for now).